Praise for *Missing May:*

★ "We're in with these people too deep to put the story down. We just can't make ourselves leave them."—*Booklist*, Starred Focus review

◆ "A beautifully written, life-affirming book."—*Kirkus Reviews*, Pointer

★ "[Rylant's] tightly woven plot wastes no words . . . a tribute to a fine writer who brings to the task a natural grace of language, an earthly sense of humor, and a well-grounded sense of the spiritual."—*School Library Journal*, Starred

★ ". . . will touch readers to tears."—*Bulletin of the Center for Children's Books*, Recommended

"Rylant brings insight and acceptance to an odd collection of characters we will come to love very much."—*The New York Times Book Review*

"Haunting . . . compelling."—*The Horn Book Magazine*

Cynthia Rylant is the author of many distinguished books for young readers. She lives in Eugene, Oregon.

YEARLING BOOKS are designed especially to entertain and enlighten young people. Patricia Reilly Giff, consultant to this series, received her bachelor's degree from Marymount College and a master's degree in history from St. John's University. She holds a Professional Diploma in Reading and a Doctorate of Humane Letters from Hofstra University. She was a teacher and reading consultant for many years, and is the author of numerous books for young readers.

Cynthia Rylant

MISSING MAY

A Yearling Book

Published by
Bantam Doubleday Dell Books for Young Readers
a division of
Bantam Doubleday Dell Publishing Group, Inc.
1540 Broadway
New York, New York 10036

ISBN: 0-440-40865-2

Reprinted by arrangement with Orchard Books, a division of
Franklin Watts, Inc., New York

Printed in the United States of America

October 1993

31 30 29 28 27 26 25 24 23

OPM

For MARVIN O. MITCHELL,
my most extraordinary teacher

PART ONE

Still as Night

CHAPTER ONE

When May died, Ob came back to the trailer, got out of his good suit and into his regular clothes, then went and sat in the Chevy for the rest of the night. That old car had been parked out by the doghouse for as long as I could remember, and the weeds had grown up all around it so you didn't even notice it unless you looked, and for years I couldn't understand why Ob didn't just get rid of the awful thing. Until I saw him sitting in it after the funeral. Then I knew that even though nobody in the world figured that old car had any good purpose, Ob knew there was some real reason to let it sit. And when May died, he figured out what it was.

I never saw two people love each other so

much. Sometimes the tears would just come over me, looking at the two of them, even six years back when I first got here and was too young to be thinking about love. But I guess I must have had a deep part of me thinking about it, hoping to see it all along, because the first time I saw Ob help May braid her long yellow hair, sitting in the kitchen one night, it was all I could do not to go to the woods and cry forever from happiness.

I know I must have been loved like that, even if I can't remember it. I must have; otherwise, how could I even recognize love when I saw it that night between Ob and May? Before she died, I know my mother must have loved to comb my shiny hair and rub that Johnson's baby lotion up and down my arms and wrap me up and hold and hold me all night long. She must have known she wasn't going to live and she must have held me longer than any other mother might, so I'd have enough love in me to know what love was when I saw it or felt it again.

When she died and all her brothers and sisters passed me from house to house, nobody ever wanting to take care of me for long, I still had that lesson in love deep inside me and I didn't grow mean or hateful when nobody cared enough to make me their own little girl. My poor mother had left me enough love to go on until somebody did come along who'd want me.

Then Uncle Ob and Aunt May from West Virginia visited, and they knew an angel when they saw her and they took me on home.

Home was, still is, a rusty old trailer stuck on the face of a mountain in Deep Water, in the heart of Fayette County. It looked to me, the first time, like a toy that God had been playing with and accidentally dropped out of heaven. Down and down and down it came and landed, thunk, on this mountain, sort of cockeyed and shaky and grateful to be all in one piece. Well, sort of one piece. Not counting that part in the back where the aluminum's peeling off, or the one missing window, or the front steps that are sinking.

That first night in it with Ob and May was as close to paradise as I may ever come in my life. Paradise because these two old people—who never dreamed they'd be bringing a little girl back from their visit with the relatives in Ohio—started, from the minute we pulled up in Ob's old Valiant, to turn their rusty, falling-down place into a house just meant for a child. May started talking about where they'd hang the swing as soon as she hoisted herself out of the front seat (May was a big woman), and Ob was designing a tree house in his head before he even got the car shut off. I was still so sick to my stomach from traveling all those curvy West Virginia roads that all I could do was swallow and nod, swallow and nod. Try to smile without puking.

But when we got inside the trailer, it became plain to me at once that they didn't need to do any great changing to make a little girl happy. First thing I saw when May switched on the light were those shelves and shelves—seemed every wall was covered with them—of whirligigs. I knew what they were right off even though they weren't like any whirligigs I'd ever seen. Back in Ohio people had them hooked to their fences or stuck out in their gardens to scare off the birds. And they'd be mostly the same everywhere: a roadrunner whose legs spun in the wind, or maybe a chicken or a duck. Cartoon characters were popular—Garfield was in a lot of gardens with his arms whirling like crazy in the breeze.

I'd seen plenty of whirligigs, but never any like Ob's. Ob was an artist—I could tell that the minute I saw them—though *artist* isn't the word I could have used back then, so young. None of Ob's whirligigs were farm animals or cartoon characters. They were *The Mysteries*. That's what Ob told me, and I knew just what he was talking about. One whirligig was meant to be a thunderstorm and it was so like one, black and gray, beautiful and frightening. Another was Ob's idea of heaven, and I thought his angels just might come off that thing and fly around that house trailer any minute, so golden and light were they. There was Fire and

Love and Dreams and Death. Even one called
May, which had more little spinning parts than any
of the rest of the whirligigs, and these parts all
white—her Spirit, he said. They were grounded to
a branch from an oak tree and this, he said, was
her Power.

I stood there before those shelves, watching
these wonders begin to spin as May turned on the
fan overhead, and I felt like a magical little girl, a
chosen little girl, like Alice who has fallen into
Wonderland. This feeling has yet to leave me.

And as if the whirligigs weren't enough, May
turned me to the kitchen, where she pulled open
all the cabinet doors, plus the refrigerator, and she
said, "Summer, whatever you like you can have
and whatever you like that isn't here Uncle Ob will
go down to Ellet's Grocery and get you. We want
you to eat, honey."

Back in Ohio, where I'd been treated like a
homework assignment somebody was always having to do, eating was never a joy of any kind. Every
house I had ever lived in was so particular about
its food, and especially when the food involved me.
There's no good way to explain this. But I felt like
one of those little mice who has to figure out the
right button to push before its food will drop down
into the cup. Caged and begging. That's how I felt
sometimes.

My eyes went over May's wildly colorful cab-
inets, and I was free again. I saw Oreos and Ruffles
and big bags of Snickers. Those little cardboard
boxes of juice that I had always, just once, wanted
to try. I saw fat bags of marshmallows and cans of
SpaghettiOs and a little plastic bear full of honey.
There were real glass bottles of Coke looking cold
as ice in the refrigerator and a great big half of a
watermelon taking up space. And, best of all, a
carton of real chocolate milk that said Hershey's.

Whirligigs of Fire and Dreams, glistening Coke
bottles and chocolate milk cartons to greet me. I
was six years old and I had come home.

CHAPTER TWO

*M*ay was gardening when she died. That's the word she always used: *gardening*. Everybody else in Fayette County would say they were going out to work in the garden, and that's the picture you'd get in your mind—people out there laboring and sweating and grunting in the dirt. But Aunt May *gardened*, and when she said it your mind would see some lovely person in a yellow-flowered hat snipping soft pink roses, little robins landing on her shoulders.

Of course May never owned a flowered hat in her life, and her garden was as practical as anyone else's. In place of roses it was full of thick pole beans and hard green cabbages and strong carrots. It was a reliable garden, and friendly, and both Ob and me finally thought it right that May should have flown up out of her body right there in that friendly garden, among all those cheerful vegetables, before she waved good-bye to us and went on to be that bright white Spirit Ob had known all along she was.

Only this part of her death seemed right. The garden. All the rest of it seemed so wrong, and it has been nearly six months—we have gone through two seasons—without her, and still I don't know what kind of life Ob and I are going to come up with for ourselves. We have not done much of anything since, except to miss May and hurt. I never would have thought us to be so lost. We used to be tougher than this.

Winter's not helping. February's a grim time in these mountains. It is pitch black in the morning when I set off down the mountain for the school bus, leaving Ob behind, watching me out the picture window. I feel adrift. When I was younger, either Ob or May would walk me out to the road and stand there freezing with me in the dark, making me stomp my feet to keep the blood circulating till the lights of the bus would finally bounce off the trees up the ridge and somebody could hand me over to the roaring heater of Number 56.

But now I am twelve, and expected to go it alone out to the stop. It isn't fear that this bitter

February darkness starts working up in my stomach. I never have been afraid of anything since I came to live on this mountain. It's just lonesomeness. Ob behind me all alone in that old trailer full of sleeping whirligigs, and me on this black road, and both of us needing May so much. It's worse needing somebody in the dark, in winter, of an early cold morning.

But most amazingly, most miraculously, now Ob is insisting that May was, *is*, right here with us. That she came back a few days ago and is truly right here with us.

It was on Sunday, and we were outside cutting open some milk jugs to make into bird feeders when suddenly Ob straightened up, put down his knife, and like a dog who thinks he's heard something move, pricked up his ears and listened.

"Ob?" I said.

Ob drew up his nose and got this foolish look on him, like he was about to sneeze.

"Ob?" I said again and beginning to get a little nervous.

Then his head snapped up straight like a soldier at attention and he said, "Hotdamn!"

My heart was beating fast.

"What is it, Ob?"

Ob ran his bony fingers through that last bit of hair on his head and looked down to the ground in stupefaction. He pulled a gray handkerchief from his back pocket and blew into it. Then he folded the cloth up neatly, gave his nose one more confident swipe, and jammed the hanky back in his pocket. He looked hard at me. I'd seen that look on his face before. It was the look that always announced he'd gotten some kind of revelation. Ob was a deep thinker and he was often getting revelations.

"May was with us," he said, with the same certainty he might have used telling me it was February.

"Huh?" I put down my knife beside me.

"May was right here with us, just now. I swear to God. I felt her, Summer, all up and down me like I'd just poured her in a glass and drunk her."

He stared off in the distance, shaking his head again. Ob didn't look so good. Well, he's never looked real good. Ob is one of those Ichabod Crane types in looks. May's passing had just made him look more scarecrow than ever.

But it didn't cross my mind to doubt him.

"Well, how'd she feel?" I asked him.

He looked back over at me.

"What's that?"

"How'd she *feel*?" I repeated. "Did she feel, like, light, like an angel? Did she tell you anything?"

Ob's eyes moved off to the bag of birdseed beside him as he thought. Finally he answered.

"She felt like she did when we was packing up to go to Ohio," he said.

"Like she was going to *Ohio?*" I couldn't fathom May taking the trouble of dying just so she could go to Ohio.

He slowly shook his head.

"All those years," he said, "every time we'd be packing up to go see the folks in Ohio, half of May would want to go and half of her would want to stay here. Couldn't make up her blame mind. She used to be afraid she'd lose this place if she left it for very long. Afraid it and the 'gigs would burn up or be washed away. She just didn't want to let this trailer out of her sight.

"But it kept her in a pickle because she always feared losing her Ohio kin, too. Feared one of them would up and die, unexpected, like her mommy and daddy in the flash flood, if she let them out of her sight for too long. So every so often she'd have to leave this place and go check on them."

He gave a big long sigh.

"She felt like she did when we was packing up to go to Ohio," he said simply, figuring I'd understand.

Well, I did understand, and it didn't set well with me at all. I never expected May to be back with us, and now that she'd stopped by, the least I expected of her was that she'd be able to make up her mind. I needed that from her. I needed to know that dying and going to heaven didn't involve any regrets or sorrows or worries. I wanted May to shine down on us and tell us she was having the most wonderful time, better than anything we could ever dream of. I sure didn't want her stopping by wondering if she'd done the right thing after all, and was everything unplugged and the stove turned off.

I believe in ghosts. Maybe angels would be a better word for them. But ghosts seems more to the point. So if Ob says May was here, I figure she was.

Anyway, I know May herself believed in spirits from the next world. She used to talk about her mommy and daddy watching over her after they died in the flash flood. Poor May. She was only nine when it hit. The rain came all day and all night and all the next day till finally the mountain couldn't soak up the water anymore and down it washed, down the creek bed, a solid wall of water twenty feet high, down into the valley where May and her people lay fast asleep. It hit that little valley like a tidal wave, and whole houses broke in pieces. Big trucks turned over, floated away. Trees cracked in half.

May said that her mother—May always called her Mommy—heard that awful water coming and jumped out of bed, running for May's room. She lifted little May out of her dreaming and ran and put her in the old metal washtub.

That's all May ever remembered. The next memory she had was of waking up in that tub six miles from home and pulling a tired old cat from the water she was floating in. Her mommy and daddy were gone, lost forever.

But May says they watched over her anyway. And all the rest of the time she was growing up, she'd get these strong feelings whether or not to do something, feelings that told her which way to go. These feelings kept her out of a boy's car which that night wrapped itself around a tree. They told her not to trust her weird neighbor, Mr. Rice, who the police carted off to jail. And one day they told her to stick with Ob.

May always said that once she got with Ob, her mommy and daddy could rest easy, and they finally flew off to that big church picnic in the sky. She said her daddy would be cleaning God out of his potato salad.

May was the best person I ever knew. Even better than Ob. She was a big barrel of nothing but love, and while Ob and me were off in our dreamy heads, May was here in this trailer seeing to it there was a good home for us when we were ready to land. She understood people and she let them be whatever way they needed to be. She had faith in every single person she ever met, and this never failed her, for nobody ever disappointed May. Seems people knew she saw the very best of them, and they'd turn that side to her to give her a better look.

Ob was never embarrassed about being a disabled navy man who fiddled with whirligigs all day long, and I never was embarrassed about being a kid who'd been passed around for years. We had May to brag on us both. And we felt strong.

But we're not strong anymore. And I think Ob's going to die, truly die, if I can't figure a way to mend his sorry broken heart. And if Ob does go, goes off to be with May, then it'll be just me and the whirligigs left. And all of us still as night, praying for wings, real wings, so we can fly away.

CHAPTER THREE

*I*f Cletus gets wind that May's back, I know he'll take it and run with it. The last thing Cletus needs is a ghost to dwell on. As if his strange mind didn't have enough to think about.

I swear. When Ob spotted him snooping around the old Chevy last fall, I warned Ob to have nothing to do with him. I'd been riding the school bus with Cletus for a year, since his family moved up from Raleigh County, and I had decided he was insane. Back when he first came, he had going this collection of potato chip bags. He had practically the whole school saving their Wise and Tom's and Ruffles bags for him. Heading home on the bus every day, people would be pulling flat shiny bags out of their history books like crazy and passing them to Cletus in the backseat. I didn't participate. I was certain the boy was a flat-out lunatic.

After that it was buttons. Then it was spoons. He went through a plant phase, which didn't last too long because he said his thumb just wasn't green enough. Then it was wrapping paper. Everybody who had a birthday got in touch with Cletus.

Till finally he settled into pictures, and that seems to have stuck. Everybody in seventh grade, probably everybody in Deep Water Junior High, knows about Cletus and his pictures. And ever since Cletus came snooping around Ob's old Chevy last November, Ob and me know about them, too. Only too well.

Wonder what May would think of us, sitting on the sofa, Cletus squeezed in between, and passing back and forth covers from paperback books, the front panels of cereal boxes (those with the faces), and *Life* magazine cut to shreds. We've looked at newspaper photos of the Kiwanis and those chubby little bears off herbal tea. Dream homes from real estate circulars and cats off 9-Lives.

"Anything with a story to it" is what Cletus says he's looking for. He keeps telling me I ought to be writing these stories to go with his pictures, since Mrs. Lacey at school has been bragging on those things I wrote for English. But the last thing on earth I plan to do is go digging through the pictures in Cletus's beat-up vinyl suitcase so we can *collaborate*, as he puts it. I can just see it: me and Cletus looking at the front of a cornflakes box, searching for deep meaning. Holy bejeezus.

Cletus had been investigating the Chevy because he thought there might be some old newspapers lining its floorboards. Ob looked out at him that Saturday morning after Thanksgiving (which had been a tough holiday without May) and he said, "Who is that boy?"

"That's Cletus Underwood," I answered, my mouth completely dropped open in wonder at the sight of him in our yard.

We watched Cletus try the handle of one of the back doors.

"He trying to *steal* that banged-up old thing?" Ob asked.

"Uh-uh" was all I could say.

Ob watched Cletus a while longer; then he reached for his coat on the back of a kitchen chair.

"Where you going?" I asked.

"To get acquainted," Ob answered, and he pushed open the door and went out.

Well, of course he didn't come back alone. There he was, coming in to the house with that crazy Cletus Underwood, who had fished his old suitcase from the bushes beside the Chevy and was holding it up against his chest.

"Hi, Summer!" he said with too big a smile.

I wasn't about to encourage him. "Hi," I answered dumbly, trying to look too boring to be worth staying for.

But he did. He stayed. He stayed seven solid hours. We fed him lunch just after he got here and dinner just before he left. Seven ungodly hours of crazy Cletus Underwood.

Thing was, though, Ob really liked him. I hadn't seen Ob interested in one solitary thing since May left us last summer, and here his face was kind of lit up, kind of full of interest and sparkle, as Cletus made himself at home and told us his life story in between showing us the pictures in his suitcase. It turned out that even though Ob didn't know Cletus's parents personally—them being from Raleigh County—he did know some of Cletus's Fayette County relatives and he seemed genuinely interested to know that Joe Underwood was working in a machine shop down in Durham and that Betty Underwood had dyed her blonde hair black and turned her garage into a combination ceramics shop and religious bookstore.

I found out that Cletus's parents were pretty old, nearly as old as Ob, and they didn't get out much. Maybe that's why Cletus and Ob had such an easy time of getting to be friends. Cletus was used to older people. And Ob appreciated anybody crazier than him.

We sat on the sofa looking at Cletus's pictures

while the Lawrence Welk show went on past us on the TV. All those Welk shows were really old, but people loved them, so the station kept on playing them. The only time we lifted our eyes from Cletus's suitcase was when Ob wanted to watch those two Barbie and Ken dolls dance the tango. Ob loved the tango. Cletus smiled through the whole dance and clapped his hands when it was done. Then we all went back to the pictures.

"This one here I got from the barber shop," Cletus said, pulling out a heavy piece of paper with a picture of a slick-looking man advertising Brylcreem.

"I think the story here," he explained, "is that Brylcreem guy's nerves are bad. He's always cleaning under his fingernails and tweezing out his nose hairs and picking at his teeth. Probably got a whole box of toothpicks in his glove compartment. Bet he sniffs his armpits, too."

I was speechless at all this. Just struck dumb. But not Ob. No, he was curious about this Brylcreem guy, now you mentioned it, and he took the picture from Cletus's chunky hand and studied it.

"I think you got something there," Ob told Cletus with a confident nod of his head. "Except the part about the armpits. This man's too delicate a constitution to be sniffing at his armpits. But all the rest I figure is right on the money."

It's those kinds of conversations we've been

having since November. Speculations about the armpits of Brylcreem men.

Still, I guess I am grateful for Cletus. He got Ob through an awful Christmas by bringing over a one-thousand piece jigsaw puzzle of the Great Pyramids Christmas morning. (Cletus said he and his parents ate turkey and opened all their presents on Christmas Eve and by morning the holiday was over at his house.) He got Ob to sit with him for twelve hours straight putting the puzzle together. Practically all the pieces were brown—brown pyramid, brown sand, brown people. It looked like pure torture to me. But Cletus and Ob were as enthralled as cats in front of a fish tank, so I just kept them happy by cooking five turkey TV dinners in a row and refilling their RC's. I spent the rest of my time reading one of the Phyllis Whitney paperbacks Ob got me. I can't ever get enough of Phyllis Whitney. And reading kept my mind off May.

So here we are now, two months later in the heart of dark February, with May slipping in, Ob slipping out, and Cletus and me just grabbing at anything we can save. May used to laugh about moving here to Deep Water, West Virginia. She had a helpless kind of fear about water, about rain, and she'd say God was testing her sense of humor, setting her up in a place called Deep Water. She never failed Him. May would tell strangers where she was from, and I would see her glance up at the sky with a sassy kind of grin on her face when she said the words "Deep Water." Like she was giving God a friendly nudge with her elbow.

May would tell Cletus and me, if she was here right now, that it's okay to grab for something or somebody that's being swept away from you. She'd tell us to hold on tight because we're all meant to be together. We're all meant to need each other.

She'd just remind us that there's more places to be together than this one. She'd tell us we don't have to give up if this life doesn't give us everything we want. There's always another one.

But that's where May and me always parted company. Because I never could count on another chance at happiness. When I got Ob and May after all those years of having nobody, that *was* my idea of dying and going to heaven. I never expected something that big to happen to me more than once.

Cletus says I think like a tired old woman. He says I'm going to turn into one of those green-eyed ladies at the Kmart checkout if I'm not careful.

"Summer," he said to me once, "drop some of them bricks you keep hauling around with you. Life just ain't that heavy."

I think I must have got old and heavy when

May left us. Ob needed somebody to fill the empty hole she left, and I reckon I thought if I aged about fifty years, I might could fill it for him.

But the only person who seems to be giving Ob anything these days is crazy Cletus. And now, if she plans to stay a while, May.

CHAPTER FOUR

"*L*ook here at this."

I reached across the aisle of the school bus and took what Cletus was handing me.

It was an old photograph, fading away like a dawn that leaves you little by little, and it was of a child. A baby in a flowing white gown, arranged on a tall chair out in the middle of a field. The baby's gown was draped so that the chair was practically invisible, and the only thing you saw was this child hovering in midair, looking at the camera.

"Weird," I said, handing it back.

"I think something like this ought to be in a museum," Cletus said, pushing a greasy strand of hair back from his eyes. Cletus's black hair is long, straight, and, from my point of view, slimy. I don't think Cletus bathes much, though he never exactly stinks. He just seems to me the type who'd layer on the Right Guard for days before he'd finally break down and take a shower.

"It's what they call *surreal*," he went on. "Taking something real and sort of stretching it out like a piece of taffy into a thing that's true but distorted. You know. Like old lady Henley's face-lift."

I smiled. Mrs. Henley was our seventh grade art teacher who just couldn't handle getting old. She was the only person in Deep Water who'd ever had a face-lift—went off to Charleston to get it—and anybody from out of town could have guessed it. She just had this look on her, like she was going to spring loose all of a sudden and snap clear across to the other side of town.

"Where'd you get it?" I asked, leaning over to take another look at the photograph.

"I was up at Mrs. Davis's house, seeing if she needed anything from the store. I showed her my suitcase, and she brought me in and pulled a great big box off the top shelf of her closet. It was crammed full of stuff like this. I thought I'd struck gold."

"She gave you that picture?"

Cletus nodded. "I was dying to take home

every one of them, but I didn't say nothing. Just picked through the lot like I was sampling chocolates from a box.

"I stayed on for hours in her living room, going through all those pictures. I don't think she planned on giving me any, but finally I guess she figured it was the only way to get rid of me. So she let me take this one."

I stared at the floating baby.

"Did she choose it, or you?"

"I did. It was just too surreal to pass up."

I shook my head.

"I can't believe you planted yourself in that old lady's house like some fungus mold till you got a picture out of her."

Cletus took one last look at the photograph, then stuck it inside his math book.

"Aw, she had a good time. She don't ever get any company."

I shook my head again in disapproval. I'm always shaking my head at Cletus. As if I have some need to keep reminding him that his presence in my life is something I neither intended nor arranged.

"So how's Ob?" Cletus asked.

I thought of Ob, this particular cold morning, not even bothering to fix his usual cup of cocoa when he got out of bed. He made sure I was up, and had my lunch fixed, and was out the door on time. But he didn't have his cocoa.

"Fair," I answered.

Cletus looked longer at me, maybe hoping he could fathom Ob by seeing him inside my eyes. But I didn't have any deep truths to tell Cletus about Ob. Well . . . none except that visit from May, and Cletus wasn't about to get that out of me.

Which didn't matter anyway because he got it straight from the horse's mouth that very night after supper.

"You believe in an afterlife, Cletus?" Ob asked, handing Cletus a cup of black coffee. Cletus had dropped by on his way home from prayer meeting. Cletus told us he didn't go there for prayer. He went there for the doughnuts they always had after the service.

I looked up from the paper on women suffragettes I was writing for history and held my breath.

"Sure, I do," Cletus answered, sipping at the coffee, a strand of his stringy hair nearly dunking itself. "Even been there once."

Ob's face lit up just as mine went dark.

"You don't say," Ob answered.

"I was maybe seven years old," Cletus began to explain as he settled himself back into the La-Z-Boy. "My grandpa had been real sick and he'd finally died the night before. Next day people were preparing for the funeral and ignoring me in their bereavement, so I just decided to go on down to the river by myself, thinking I'd skip some stones till everything had passed over.

"Well, I'm standing there on the riverbank skipping rocks when next thing I know I'm drowning. I mean *drowning*. My foot must have slipped or something, and in I went. And I never was able to swim a lick.

"And here's the God's truth, Ob. . . ."

Ob set down his coffee cup and straightened up to listen.

"I passed on. I did. I remember this light ahead of me and reaching out to it. I went after it, and suddenly everything was brilliant white and, I swear to God, my grandpa was there smiling at me and—you won't believe this part—my little dog Cicero who'd been dead three years, he was with me, too."

Cletus stopped talking long enough to take a few gulps of his coffee, and while he drank, Ob and me had our eyes glued to him like a bomb set to explode. Nobody said a word, waiting.

"So I'm there hugging Grandpa and petting little Cicero and feeling just fantastic when I hear this voice say, 'Cletus, go on home now.' I swear that's what it said. Told me to go on home.

"And Grandpa and Cicero started fading away and this awful coldness and heaviness come over me, like I was wrapped in sopping wet rugs, and next thing I know I'm there throwing up like crazy and my uncle Willy is threatening to beat me to death for nearly drowning."

Cletus grinned at us both.

Hell, I thought miserably.

"Heaven!" Ob said out loud. "You went to heaven and back, Cletus!"

Cletus nodded his head.

"No doubt in my mind," he answered.

"Then maybe it's you who can talk to May for me. She's been trying to reach me, but I ain't too good at communicating on her new wavelength. I need me an interpreter."

Cletus gaped at Ob.

"You heard from *May?*"

"Couple of times," Ob said.

A couple of times? I had known only about the one time, the first time, when I was there, making bird feeders. It suddenly hurt me that Ob hadn't told me about the second—and that now he was revealing everything to Cletus instead of me. I felt more than ever cut apart from him, sent off on my own while he took off on his, while he made plans to set aside this life we both knew so purely to try to make it to another one he knew nothing about except that somewhere in it he might find May. I didn't know how to keep him tied to me. Already he was starting to live among the dead.

"Well, I'm no psychic or nothing," Cletus told Ob. "I feel a connection to the spirit world because I've been there—sort of like remembering a place where you once went on vacation. But I never get any supernatural messages or anything. I don't know any ghosts—personally, I mean."

Ob shook this off.

"Don't matter. You must have something special about you, if you've been over to the other side. Maybe just having you in the house'll help."

Holy crap, I thought. The last thing I wanted was for Cletus to have an excuse to hang out at the trailer any more than he already did. Now Ob wanted to keep Cletus here like he was installing some afterlife antenna on the place.

"But May didn't even know Cletus," I said lamely, making a puny attempt at party pooping.

Ob smiled at Cletus and patted him on the knee.

"She don't have to meet him in the flesh to know this boy, Summer," he said, looking at Cletus's interested face. "May's been looking at them pictures over our shoulders all along. She knows Cletus, and I'll betcha she even knows his little dog."

Ob's smile then slowly disappeared, and he wiped a hand across his eyes. In an instant he looked more tired than I'd ever seen him, and my heart sank.

Cletus and I just looked at each other.

CHAPTER FIVE

*T*he first thing Ob did when the after-life antenna came around again was to take him out into May's empty garden. It was a pitiful sight, the three of us in our overcoats and boots, standing among the dead stalks of winter, hoping for a sign of life from the woman who once had kept everything alive on that soil. Including some of us.

I really didn't expect May to show up, but Ob's enthusiasm was so desperate, so sincere in its belief in miracles, that a part of me held out just a little hope that she might fly her soft spirit over us and come gently into our midst. May had never let us down when she was alive, she'd never not shown up when she was supposed to be somewhere, and it was the memory of her reliableness, I guess, that fueled our wide-eyed optimism.

What Cletus thought about it all I can't imagine. For once he was quiet, let Ob do all the talking and explaining, and like a little child let himself be led among the dead beans and broccoli toward the heart of a woman he never even met.

Ob must have thought that by talking about May there in that place, painting her before Cletus's ignorant eyes, he could flood the garden with the vibrations needed to draw her to us. Like that old joke of talking about someone till his ears burn.

So there we stood, hands dug deep in our pockets, Ob looking at Cletus, Cletus looking up at the sky, and me looking down at the ground. Ob talked about what a good wife May was and all the sweet things she'd done for him—for us—while she was living. I was kind of surprised at the things Ob picked to talk about. I figured he'd choose the big ones—like her secretly saving up for three years in a row to buy him that expensive plane saw he was coveting over at Sears. Or the year she stayed awake thirty-two hours straight when fever from the chicken pox had me full of delirium, so sick I wanted to die.

But these heroic gestures of hers were ignored, and he chose instead to mention the simpler things:

how she had rubbed down his ailing knee with Ben-Gay every single night, not missing a one, so he might be able to stand on that leg when he got out of bed the next morning. The way she had called to me through the window when I was little and playing on the swing set, saying, "Summer honey, you are the *best* little girl I ever did know," then going back to whatever she was doing. (I had not remembered this about her until that moment.) And a series of other sweetnesses that Ob had obviously cradled in his memory, looking for some way to bring them to life.

Cletus watched the sky and glanced at Ob now and then, nodding his head to let Ob know he was listening. Cletus was wearing his hat with the fake fur earflaps, and once I got a crazy urge to giggle when I thought of those flaps flapping and Cletus rising up like Charlie Brown's Snoopy and flying across the garden and away.

But his hat behaved itself, and he stood patiently, allowing Ob to say all he needed to say. It almost felt like a funeral, like we'd just buried some beloved pet in the cold ground of the garden, and in some ways, it was more comfort, more *real*, to me than May's true funeral had been. Seems once people bring in outsiders who make a career of bereavement—undertakers, preachers—their grieving gets turned into a kind of system, like the way everybody lines up the same way to go in to a movie or sits the same way in a doctor's office. All Ob and me wanted to do when we lost May was hold on to each other and wail in that trailer for days and days. But we never got the chance, because just like there are certain ways people expect you to get married, or go to church, or raise kids, there are certain ways people expect you to grieve. When May died, Ob and me had to talk business with the funeral parlor, religion with the preacher, and make small talk with dozens of relatives and people we'd hardly ever seen before. We had to eat their food. We had to let them hug us. We had to see them watching our faces for any sign of a nervous breakdown.

May's funeral turned Ob and me into temporary sort-of socialites, and we never really got the chance to howl and pull our hair out. People wanted us to grieve proper.

So standing there in that bleak and empty garden listening to Ob make May alive again, that seemed to fix something in me that had needed fixing ever since the funeral. And in the oddest way Cletus became what we'd needed all along from the undertaker and preacher and visiting relatives. He became the perfect consoler, because he listened to every word Ob said and kept his fat mouth shut. Cletus had some gifts—I was learning this bit by bit—and knowing when to talk and when not to was turning out to be one of them.

Ob finally drained his cup of praises to May and grew still. His eyes looked with Cletus's to the sky, and I couldn't keep mine from following. Nothing but a black crow passed overhead. And no sound but Ob's heavy breathing and an occasional snort from Cletus, whose nose had started to run.

Neither Cletus nor I was willing to make a move until Ob did. We watched him turn his head this way and that, like adjusting the dial on a radio. Then finally he gave a great sigh, and we knew May had not come to him. He shook his head wearily and walked away from us toward the empty trailer.

We watched him go over the hill and through the front door. Then we looked at each other and we, too, let out our own sighs of disappointment.

"He's going to make himself sick or crazy, one," I said to Cletus, suddenly feeling a big lump in my throat, a wetness in my eyes.

Cletus shrugged his shoulders and gave me one of his strange smiles.

"Least it gives him something to do," he said. "Gets him out of bed in the mornings."

I shook my head and remained silent. I didn't want Cletus to know the pain this caused me, that

I wasn't enough to bring Ob to life each day. That it wasn't enough he had me left to still love.

Cletus looked at me.

"You don't really believe he feels her, do you?" he said, almost like he was accusing me of something.

I gave him a sharp look.

"Why? What's it to you whether I believe it or don't?"

Cletus shrugged his shoulders.

"Ain't nothing to me. I just figured you to have more imagination than that, you being a writer and all."

"I'm not any writer."

"Oh, the heck you're not," Cletus answered with a look of total impatience.

"Cletus, don't preach at me." I was beginning to think I might yell or cry and I didn't want to do either. What I wanted was for him to stop pushing at me.

He looked off toward the woods.

"That's probably what she gave him," he said matter-of-factly.

I straightened up.

"What? What did she give him?"

Cletus squatted down to pick at a dry broccoli leaf.

"Well, you know Ob won't just make a whirligig from something we can understand. He don't carve out little doggies and kitties. Because he don't care about things *concrete*. Ob's not making yard decorations. He's making art. I can understand why he never put the 'gigs out in the yard. He never meant to entertain the neighbors.

"I just figure May gave him permission to have some imagination."

Cletus looked up at my face.

"Ob's got visions, Summer. Just like you, except you're always fighting yours off."

And when Cletus said that, I felt like I couldn't ever win anymore, I couldn't ever come out on top of anything in this life. I couldn't even remember what it was about Cletus I used to hate so much. I couldn't even stay ahead of him.

I turned and walked away. I felt lost. I might as well have been spinning in a round metal tub, in a twenty-foot wall of water, washing down off that mountain. Just lost forever in Deep Water.

PART TWO

Set Free

CHAPTER SIX

I did not stay lost for long.

Guidance came to me in the form of a greasy-haired lunatic, and now, desperate, I am passing him the torch, hoping he can lead us out of this infernal darkness, this place none of us can anymore call home.

The day after May failed to make her appearance, the day after Ob trudged miserably one way while I trudged miserably the other, was what they call in English class the *dénouement*. All our stories took a sharp turn because of what happened that next day, we were put on a different road, and like Dorothy, the Scarecrow, and the Cowardly Lion, we are all hoping that there really is a wizard of Oz. And that in that Emerald City we will find what it is Ob needs to finally rest his soul.

The day after May didn't come to us, Ob didn't get out of bed. He didn't get me up either, and from a bad dream I woke with a start, knowing things were wrong, knowing I had missed something vitally important.

Among these, of course, was the school bus. It was Monday, and Ob should have called me out of bed at five-thirty, but he didn't, and when I finally woke at seven o'clock, it was too late to set the day straight. But maybe God intended for me to sieep in that morning, needed me to stay home, as He counted on all of the day's events spreading out just like He'd planned them.

I jumped from bed and hurried down the hall to Ob's room at the other end of the trailer.

I knocked on his door.

"Ob?"

No answer came to me.

"Ob? You awake?"

My breathing was tight, just like my nerves, as I wondered what I'd find inside that room. I had been dreading Ob's death for so long that in my mind I practically had the coffin picked out and which tie he'd wear. I thought this morning might be the one for truly final decisions.

"Summer?" I heard him say in a weak voice.

My heart lifted a little at the sound of his voice, and I opened the door a crack. There still wasn't much light outside, so all I could see of him was his thin, bony silhouette upright in the bed. I could feel the fear in him.

"Ob, you okay?" I went over and reached out to touch his arm. "Are you sick, Ob?"

His hand came up and covered mine. He was shaking his head, patting my fingers again and again. I wasn't sure what to do.

I sat down on the edge of the bed. His face was gray in the light, and he looked to me like some poor victim of a medical experiment.

"What is it, Ob?" I asked.

And in that gray cast, that fog in which we both sat, I could see, and feel, that tears were rolling down his face.

"I must've overslept," he whispered.

And he knew, as well as I, that he had never, not any day of his life, overslept. He was as trust-worthy as the sun in this.

I took my hand from underneath his and stroked his shoulder.

"It's all right, Ob," I told him. "Happens to everybody," I said, knowing full well it didn't.

"You go on back to sleep if you want, Ob. I'll put some coffee on the stove. And I'll fix you some eggs and cocoa when you get up."

Ob didn't protest. He was humiliated, I knew, and wanted to be left alone.

I understood that feeling. Once when I was in fourth grade, our teacher had made us write descriptions of each other. She said she would read them aloud and we would try to guess who was being described.

One of the descriptions she read was of a girl who sounded to me like some sad welfare case, in the sorry way her clothes and hair were described. But everyone in the class seemed to know right away who it was. Only the girl herself was stumped.

That was about the only time in my life I didn't put two and two together. And once I realized the writer had in fact been describing me—or what she saw when she looked at me—all I wanted was to be home, safe with May and Ob, never to leave the haven of my own room again.

But I had to sit among others for the rest of the school day. Exposed.

I understood Ob's need to be alone.

I went out to the kitchen and called the junior high to let them know I wouldn't be coming anytime that day, and I got a pot of coffee brewing. I thought about old Number 56, knew it would have sat idling a few extra minutes this morning, waiting to see if I was going to come hauling it over the hill with my coat half on and my books sliding every which way. It was a nice feeling, the knowing that I was always expected.

I sat down with my coffee and wished I had a medical book in the house, something that might give me some clues on how to help Ob. But all we had was Aunt May's worn-out copy of Dr. Spock's *Baby and Child Care*, which she had reached for every time I threw up as a child. I didn't figure on Dr. Spock giving me any good advice about old men who couldn't go on without their wives.

I watched the "Today" show a while. I even had this crazy hope that maybe I'd be lucky and Dr. Art Ulene would talk about that very thing, about grieving old men who were starting to oversleep in the mornings. But the subject was acne—which I was sorry Cletus wasn't around to hear—and I was left with nothing to go on except my own common sense.

And my own common sense was sending me a pretty strong message, one that at first I didn't want to listen to because it scared me so. But by 9:00 A.M. I had pretty much come to the conclusion that Ob had overslept not because he had made a mistake but because deep down he was finished. Finished waiting for May and finished waiting for all his grief to dry up and leave him. And maybe, in a way, finished with me.

Presently Ob did come shuffling out of his room. He was in his pajamas, hadn't even bothered to get dressed, and this sent four-alarm chills running through my whole body. He looked ready for the nursing home or the grave. My heart was breaking in half, and at the same time I was so mad at him I wanted to kill him. What was it going to take to shake some life back in him?

Ob drank his cocoa and looked out the front window while I got the table spread. It was nearly ten o'clock, and I was starving. I was used to having breakfast at five forty-five. May had always made a big hot breakfast for me. Since she died, Ob had given me cereal and toast. Today, I was cooking for myself.

Once we got settled down and began to eat, though, things relaxed a little between us and we began to talk.

I searched for topics that had generally interested both of us before, like whether or not we should get a dog and did we think that young guy at the hardware was drunk or just had a speech problem and maybe this spring we ought to buy one of those Weed Eaters so we could clean out that mess around the old Chevy.

But right in the middle of my little speech on the virtues of Weed Eaters, Ob pushed away his half-eaten breakfast and gave me a long sad look.

I shut up.

"Summer," he said, "I don't know that I can do it."

"Do what, Ob?"

He shook his head. Those tears were coming back to him.

"I never was no hand at housekeeping. Maybe there was a time I could've learned. But it's too late for me now, and I don't know that I can do all that needs to be done to keep this place running."

I knew he meant me—he meant keep me running. The trailer could take care of itself. He wasn't so sure I could.

"I can take care of myself, Ob."

He swallowed hard and waited a minute to collect his voice.

"May wouldn't have wanted you caring for yourself, child. We brought you to this place to raise you up with our own hands, and she wouldn't want you having to look to your own needs. She'd want you to have somebody right here seeing after you.

"I don't know that this old man is going to be of any use to you, Summer. I'm not doing so good since she passed on."

In a strange and unexpected way Ob's saying this exhilarated me. I'm not sure what it was, but it had something to do with him still being rooted enough to things to know when they were going wrong. If Ob had overslept and sat around in his pajamas all day and made excuses for it—or worse, thought nothing of it at all—that would have made me ready to give up on him.

But he knew he wasn't doing so good and he still knew enough to be ashamed.

That gave me some hope.

"Ob." I reached for his hand. "Maybe you could start a new batch of 'gigs. Maybe you need to get busy on something a while till some more time passes. I can take care of things. I can run this place till you're better."

He gave me a weary smile.

"There's nothing in this old head of mine to make a 'gig from, sweetheart. Seems all it's filled up with is talking to May and thinking about her dying on us. I keep running through that garden over and over, finding the poor thing and feeling my heart freeze up just like it did that day. It's over and done with except in my head, but I just can't get it out of there. I got no 'gigs in me anymore. The only vision I've got is of my poor old May, and seems there's nobody nor nothing can distract me from that. And I ain't even so sure I want to be distracted. I got to keep her with me somehow."

I nodded my head and stroked his arm. What could I say to him? He was telling the pure truth, I knew, and I didn't have any answers for either of us. All I could do was fix him another cup of cocoa and pour me another cup of coffee and just sit.

Then at three twenty-five Cletus Underwood and his suitcase showed up at the front door, and we finally got some directions to Oz.

CHAPTER SEVEN

"It's called a what kind of church?" Ob said as he looked over Cletus's shoulder at the newspaper clipping that had been pulled from the famous suitcase.

"Spiritualist," Cletus said. "The Spiritualist Church of Glen Meadows, it says right here. Over in Putnam County."

The two of them sat down on the couch while I took the La-Z-Boy, wondering to myself whether Cletus wasn't just some alien pretending to be a human life. Surely he knew he'd never get Ob and me inside of a church, even if it served a thousand different kinds of doughnuts.

Ob took the clipping from Cletus's hand while Cletus went on talking.

"The pastor there, it says, can communicate

with the dead. Says that's what the whole church is about. Making connections between this world and the other side. This isn't any ordinary church.

"I clipped this out of the paper last year because I loved that picture of her. 'The Reverend Miriam B. Young: Small Medium at Large.' Don't you just love that? I'd dearly love to write newspaper titles when I'm grown. Anyway, some call her the Bat Lady because she keeps bats as pets. Others call her the White Lady because she only wears white."

Cletus beamed at Ob.

"But I'm calling her the Just-in-Time Lady because that's what she is. She's showed up here in my suitcase just in time to lead us to May."

Ob didn't smile back. I knew he was thinking, thinking of a kind way to let Cletus know that this new idea ranked right up there with the one that gave us Cheez Whiz, and that instead of heading to Putnam County Cletus had better get himself checked into the Pineville Sanatorium.

"How long a drive you figure it is over to that part of Putnam County?" Ob finally said.

"Ob!" I shouted. "Are you crazy? We can't go to Putnam County looking for Bat Woman!"

Ob and Cletus just stared at me.

"How come we can't?" Ob asked. "You got something better to do for school break?"

"School break? We're going to spend school

break in Putnam County? In some Spiritual church?"

"Spiritualist," Cletus corrected.

"Hell, why not," Ob said, looking at Cletus with a grin. "We just might learn us a thing or two."

I saw that grin on his face, that glint in his eyes, and I knew that Ob had suddenly found himself a reason to get out of bed on time in the mornings, at least for a little while longer. The three of us might look like complete pure fools tracking down this preacher lady and her bats. But if it kept Ob grinning and chasing after some hope, I knew I'd have to be willing to follow him.

"Three hours," Cletus said.

"Say what?" Ob said.

"I figure on three hours to get there," Cletus continued. "I already looked at the map. It's an easy drive. We can take the turnpike almost all the way in. Maybe we can even stop in Charleston and look at the capitol on our way back. I've not ever been to the capitol. Never been anywhere, really, except the middle part of Raleigh County and the middle part of Fayette County. Hard to be a Renaissance Man when you can't get your nose any further than that."

"A what kind of a man?" asked Ob.

"Renaissance. Learned it in history. Back in Europe there were these men who were real well-rounded. You know, they could paint, play music, write poems. They could talk science and philosophy. Knew a lot about a lot. Folks called them Renaissance Men."

Cletus got this cocky little look on his face.

"I'm training to be one of them," he said with a big grin. "Deep Water needs itself some Renaissance Men."

"Ha!" Ob laughed and slapped Cletus on the knee. "After our little trip, you might be calling yourself a Rent-a-Séance Man!"

Both of them burst out laughing while I just sighed and went to the refrigerator to pull out some Cokes. I could tell Cletus was going to be with us a while.

He hung on till suppertime. Then when it became apparent Ob and I were probably going to rely on peanut butter to pull us through, he finally got the notion to go on home.

Cletus never once asked why I wasn't at school that day. Never once commented on Ob being in his pajamas.

He sure had some gifts.

May would have liked him. She would have said he was "full of wonders," same as Ob. May always liked the weird ones best, the ones you couldn't peg right off. She must be loving it up in heaven, where I figure everybody must just let loose. That's got to be at least one of the benefits of heaven—never having to act normal again.

Ob and I agreed to meet Cletus at his house on

Saturday, so Ob could meet Cletus's parents and get the go-ahead for Cletus to come with us to Putnam County next week. Pretty soon we'll all be in Ob's Valiant, traveling like wise men to Bethlehem, looking for that star in the sky that might point us to May.

I'm afraid. Already I've lost many things, important things, and I don't want to lose more in Putnam County. Cletus seems always to live full of hope and confidence. He thinks he's found an answer for Ob and now all we have to do is get ourselves heading out the turnpike to pick it up.

But I've got too much to lose if this Bat Lady turns out to be a hoax. If May decides not to fly along with us, if she doesn't show up in Putnam County and say whatever it is Ob needs, for life, to hear, then I figure there'll be no use us returning to our home in Deep Water. Because we will have waded out too far, out past the point of no return, too far to ever make it home again.

Cletus had sure better be right about this.

CHAPTER EIGHT

*M*ay liked bats. Maybe it was some kind of a sign that we were headed for another woman who liked them, too.

We used to get bats in the trailer. Nearly one a week when it was hibernating time. I'd wake in the night and hear that cottony flapping coming from the living room. I'd lie there a few minutes, enjoying, in a way, the strangeness of my situation; then I'd groan and drag myself up to get Ob and May. I had to walk through the living room to do it, and with the low ceiling of the trailer, the bat and I would be practically eye to eye. But I was never afraid. I was being raised by one person who liked these creatures and another who tolerated them. I had no reason to fear bats, and as I grew and discovered how many people are deathly afraid of them, it made me wonder about fear. Whether it all just starts with the people who raise us.

May would be the first out, standing in the living room and talking to the distressed bat: "Poor little feller. Must be scared to death. You never meant to come into this old trailer. . . ."

Ob would stagger out behind, rubbing his eyes and waking himself up with a few choice swear words. Ob always said cussing was like taking a strong drink of whiskey. It thawed him out and got his engine running again.

Then Ob and May would take turns trying to throw a blanket over the bat while it swooped around their heads, and pretty soon one of them would be carrying the blanket outside and watching the soft black thing fly off into the night.

Once May injured a bat by mistake, crushing it when she opened a window it had roosted on.

She thought she might save it. She put it in a box full of warm towels, and inside the box she placed a little saucer of banana pieces and some dead grubs Ob had dug out of the backyard for it. The three of us took turns the following week, looking in on it, seeing whether it had eaten anything. Once, when I checked, it had pulled itself over to the saucer and, with what seemed to be the last bit of strength it had, was licking one of the pieces of banana. The bat was so small and lovely, a little animal with wings, and I wanted it to live. But the next morning it was dead, and we buried it in May's garden.

Finally Ob had somebody check the trailer, and when we learned that the bats were flying in through the heating ducts, Ob covered these with wire and we no longer set free, or buried, any lost and lonely bats.

Ob got out of bed on time the rest of the week. And as I ate my cereal and drank my coffee before heading off to school, he would sit at the kitchen table, studying the road atlas he'd spread open, or thumb through the Triple A travel guide to West Virginia and Ohio. I didn't ask him what he was looking for. I had a feeling it wasn't anything you could find on a map.

Then Saturday morning rolled around, and we found ourselves shivering on Cletus Underwood's front porch, knocking to be let in.

Cletus's house was tiny and brown, not much bigger than some people's garages. It sat far back from the road in a clump of pine trees and to a child might have been the house where Goldilocks met the three bears. In the cold of February it looked brittle and tight, and when I saw it I had a strange urge to throw a blanket over it and warm its insides.

Ob said nothing about the place except that he

used to go fishing with a man who lived in it years ago. He said it was a good little house.

The front door opened to us, and standing there was Cletus. And I knew, in an instant, that this was not the same boy who had been coming to us with his battered old suitcase all these weeks. This was a different boy, and I knew, even before I set one foot inside his house, that here in this place, he was a much-loved boy. It's funny, how you can know something like that right away. How you can see in someone's face that he feels completely safe, and full of power and love, and suddenly things between you become so easy. Cletus was home, and he didn't need to be crazy at all. He smiled his big smile, and for the first time in my life I was glad to see him.

"Come on in, folks," he said, moving out of our way and motioning us inside. Behind him stood his parents.

I knew right off that they were shy, and unused to company. And they were older than I ever expected.

Mrs. Underwood looked to be made of dried-out apples. She was small and tight and dry, just like her house, but with a shine that attracted me. She shook my hand, and her thin cool fingers felt like twigs that could be snapped in a minute. I had a pang of fear that she might die soon. I seemed destined to be surrounded by people on their way out.

"Well, hello, Summer. It's good to finally meet you," she said softly.

"Thanks. You, too," I answered, feeling awkward before her good manners.

Mr. Underwood was shaking Ob's hand and laughing at something Ob had said. Leave it to Ob to walk right in and have the house laughing.

I loved Mr. Underwood from the minute I set eyes on him. He was a stooped-over little man with a long gray beard. A little elf. Even his cheeks were rosy. And instead of shaking my hand, he put his arm around me and gave me a squeeze and said, "We were wondering when that boy of ours was going to bring you on over here. We've been asking him since Christmas."

I stood there in his father's arms and looked to Cletus in embarrassment. I could guess now why Cletus had never had me to his house before. I had thought all along that it had something to do with his parents. That he was hiding them from me, maybe ashamed of them in some way.

Now, meeting these sweet people, I knew right away it wasn't them Cletus was ashamed of. It was me. Ashamed of me and my indifference to him, afraid to let his parents see the way I barely tolerated their strange son. Ashamed of the difference between their adoration of him and my disgust.

I had not been in that house for five minutes yet, and already I'd learned so much.

We all sat down in the little living room. Mrs. Underwood brought out an extra chair from the kitchen.

Never one to mess around, Ob got right to the point.

"Well, you know, we was wondering if you might let us take your boy Cletus along on our little trip next week."

The Underwoods both nodded and said nothing, waiting for Ob to fill in the details, which I figured he had come prepared to do. I waited to see how he would handle it.

He went on:

"See, I lost my wife last August and since then Summer, she's had a rough time of it." He looked at me and shook his head sadly. "Poor little thing. She just can't figure what to do with herself when she's got some time on her hands. So I was thinking she'd get a lot out of this little sightseeing trip."

I looked at Ob in astonishment. He avoided my eyes and continued.

"I thought we'd go on over to Putnam County to visit an old friend of mine. . ."

At least he's got that part right, I thought.

"And then go on into Charleston to see the capitol. That's where your boy comes in."

Mrs. Underwood gave Cletus an affectionate look.

"As you all know by now," Ob continued, "Cletus is a boy just full of curiosity about the world, and I reckoned maybe he'd like a chance to see the capitol, too. And him and Summer, they get on real good, they're practically best friends, and it'd be a help to her to have him along. Take her mind off things."

Ob sent me a look of deepest sympathy as I gaped back at him, while Mr. and Mrs. Underwood turned their understanding faces upon mine, probably searching for the right words to say to the poor lost child sitting before them.

Cletus had simply stared with his mouth hanging ever since Ob passed the "poor little thing" part. It was one of those rare occasions when he was too flabbergasted to speak. Like me, Cletus must have expected Ob would explain about the Bat Lady, about our real reason for going to Putnam County. He didn't know, though, how slick Ob could be. And now I had a hunch Cletus's admiration for Ob had just shot up about ten points.

Mr. Underwood was the first to reply.

"Why, sure, Ob, if you don't think Cletus'll be too much trouble to you. I know Cletus has been wanting to travel some, see new things. But I've got down in my back, and Margradel's right eye has nearly gone blind on her, and we just can't do like we used to."

I looked at Cletus to see if all this talk of illness and deterioration affected him the way it did me. But there was no fear or worry in his face. He looked perfectly serene. I couldn't understand that kind of peace. Already I was thinking I ought to get Mr. Underwood into Fayetteville to a chiropractor and maybe there was some kind of medicine that might save Mrs. Underwood's right eye. Already I was making plans on how to keep them both from the grave.

Mrs. Underwood spoke next, looking at me.

"I'm sorry about your loss, dear. It's so hard when the Lord takes a loved one away from us."

Something caught in my throat all of a sudden, and I didn't try to answer her. I was feeling way too vulnerable in the face of such tenderness. I couldn't risk opening my mouth to speak of May.

Somehow the topic turned to lighter things, and Ob and Mr. Underwood talked of the weather and the new bridge being built down the road. Mr. Underwood said he had been a machinist in his day, holding up a hand with two fingers missing to prove it. I was afraid Ob might try to top this and start pulling down his pants to show where he'd been shot in the navy in World War II. Japanese shrapnel had got him in the thigh. But he kept his head about him, and his pants around him, and I breathed a sigh of relief.

Mrs. Underwood brought us all some ginger-bread cake and the best coffee I ever tasted. She tried to get me to drink a glass of milk, couldn't get over a girl my age loving coffee so much. But Cletus told her that coffee had made me tough, and besides that all writers needed something to see them through those long novels, and better it was coffee than Jim Beam whiskey.

Mrs. Underwood's eyes crinkled in amusement as she refilled my cup.

While we sat eating, I looked around the house as much as I could. It was neat as a pin. Simple pieces of furniture, plain lamps, and only a few things on the walls. One of these was a picture of Mr. and Mrs. Underwood holding a small baby between them. It made me think about the difference between Cletus and me. About the way he could trust things to be all right. The way I worried about losing everything.

Those two people in that picture had been holding Cletus between them, frail as they were, ever since Cletus took his first breath. And Cletus just never expected them to let him fall.

During our visit, Cletus didn't pull out his old suitcase, didn't entertain us with his usual stories of exaggeration and gossip. He sat listening and looking and smiling, and I wondered what he thought of us all.

Maybe he really was wise in a different way. Maybe drowning was the best thing that ever happened to him.

I just wished May had turned around and come back from heaven the way he did.

Ob and I left the Underwood house full of warm cake and coffee. And something else. We couldn't say what. But the rest of the day had a nice quietness about it, and we laughed together about Ob's fear of telling the Underwoods the real truth ("Not everybody is as free minded as us, Summer," he said), and we began to gather up our things to take to Putnam County.

CHAPTER NINE

"Is that all you're taking?"

I looked at the grocery bag in Cletus's left hand and the famous suitcase in his right.

"Well, I would've packed my Cadillac, but I couldn't fit it in the bag," he said.

"You two stop that jawing and get on in the car," Ob said cheerfully as he slammed the trunk. "We got us an appointment in the next world."

Ob and I climbed in the front seat of the Valiant (I wasn't about to let Cletus take my front seat) and Cletus settled himself into the back, where right off he started unloading some magazines from his suitcase.

I turned around to glance over the titles and gave him a weird enough look that he had to say something.

"This old fellow up in Creasy's Hollow . . . he gave me these. They've been sitting in his out-house for a good ten years or more."

Just as I was about to puke, Ob spoke up.

"Best reading I ever done was in my daddy's old johnnyhouse. And I don't mean dirty stuff, nei-ther. He kept him some books on auto mechanics, fishing, Civil War—you name it. I used to love to get the diarrhea."

And with that our trip to Putnam County was launched.

You would have thought with two big talkers like Cletus and Ob in the car, we'd have been a noisy bunch all the way down the road.

But as soon as we got out of Deep Water and onto the main highway, a quiet spell settled over the three of us, and the only sound was the rattle of something loose in Ob's radio. There was a feel-ing in that car, and it was almost sadness, but it wasn't. It was sweeter than sadness. I knew Ob's silence was connected to May. Probably he was praying to her all the way to Putnam County, pray-ing to her to come back to him and tell him what to do now without her. For all his pep, I knew Ob was scared.

And Cletus. Well, a couple of times I looked back and saw him staring up at the tops of the mountains, staring like he was looking at angels flying up there, and his face was so clear and open that he seemed like a tiny child to me. What was it he was thinking, looking up like that?

My own quietness, I think it came from peace. Nothing needed doing in that car. Ob was beside me and safe. Cletus behind us content. I knew that for a good three hours we were going to be like this, no surprises, nothing gone wrong. I could look out at the mountains and the tiny little houses people had squeezed onto them. I could see the muddy old toys in the yards and the melting-away snowmen. The smoke from chimneys keeping people warm and happy. Dogs chained to their houses, asleep in soggy yards. I didn't need to take care of anything or anybody, and the silence was as blessed to me as the deepest kind of sleep could have been.

When the signs on the turnpike started telling us we were coming to Charleston, Cletus became so fidgety that at first I thought we'd better find a filling station, and fast.

But when he started talking about the capitol, I knew it was only nerves.

"I never have seen it," he told Ob. "Only a black-and-white picture in our West Virginia history book. Even that knocked my socks off.

"I just think about all those important people, making laws under that gold dome. It must be to

West Virginia what the Parthenon was to the Greeks."

Cletus shook his head and stared out the window toward the Du Pont plant we were passing.

"It's got to be the greatest thing," he said, "to work in the West Virginia capitol every day."

And for a second, right then, I had this strong image of Cletus someday doing that very thing. Of his being Fayette County's elected representative to the legislature and driving over to Charleston to put his head together with other important heads and enact profound laws.

Then I remembered that he liked to eat Vienna sausages from the can and watch reruns of "Laugh-In," and came to my senses.

The green-and-white road signs kept teasing us along with mentions of Capitol Street so many miles ahead, and we strained our eyes for a glimpse of the gold-leafed dome, like Columbus looking for a continent.

Then . . . there it was, and I know it was better than all three of us figured it would be. The capitol building sprawled gray concrete like a regal queen spreading out her petticoats, and its giant dome glittered pure gold in the morning sun. I felt in me an embarrassing sense of pride that she was ours. That we weren't just shut-down old coal mines and people on welfare like the rest of the country wanted to believe we were. We were this majestic, elegant thing sitting solid, sparkling in the light.

Ob kept running the car off the road as he tried to drive and look at the same time.

"Sure is a beauty," he said as he pulled the car back into the lane for the third time.

"Sure is," I heard Cletus answer. The boy looked like he was just swallowing up the sight, gulping that capitol down as fast as he could as we moved on past it, on toward I–64. I knew he wanted to stop right then and stay there, maybe forever. Forget that Bat Lady.

Ob probably knew it, too.

"Don't you folks worry," he said. "Tomorrow when we come back this way, we're going to stop and spend the whole day wandering that place. We'll see us some historical documents and some genuine West Virginia artifacts. Then we'll go have us some lunch with the senators and maybe even the governor himself in the capitol coffee shop.

"Me and Cletus, we'll tell him how to straighten out all his mess."

So as Cletus pinned his eyes to that place he thought might just be heaven, our car kept on moving, out of view of the fine gold dome, further apart from Deep Water and the people we used to be there, on nearer Putnam County and the people we were about to become. Three visitors heading for Oz.

CHAPTER TEN

"*T*he Reverend Miriam Young has passed on, I'm afraid."

We were standing on the porch of the little blue house that used to be the Spiritualist Church of Glen Meadows when we heard these awful words. And all three of us, I'm sure, felt for a moment like just passing on with her.

We'd found the place without any trouble. Drove the main highway in, stopped at a filling station and checked a phone book, and by 10:00 A.M. we were on the Reverend Young's front porch. Or what used to be hers.

There was no sign outside the home advertising it as a church, but Ob said, getting out of the car, that it wasn't the kind of religion people necessarily

advertised. He said it wasn't what you'd call Wel-
come Wagon material. And Cletus made some joke
about the church not needing a sign anyway because everybody who was supposed to come most
likely heard of it telepathically anyway. But I
wasn't so optimistic. I was always set for failures
since May died, and I was set for this one.

"Passed on where?" Cletus asked the man like
a fool.

Smiling kindly to the imbecile in our company,
the chipmunk of a man (that's the animal he fa-
vored) said, "She died, son. Last June. She's
passed on to the Spirit World."

We three just stood there dumbfounded. We
were trying to outwit Death on this trip, rise above
it, penetrate the blockades it put up between us
and May. We were coming to Putnam County to
put Death in its place, and instead it had put us
squarely back in ours.

"So who are you?" I asked brazenly, forgetting
my manners. I had nothing left to lose anyway. I
was mad at this chipmunk and ready to fight.
Ready to squeeze that Bat Lady right out of him.

But his face never altered as he looked into my
eyes. He smiled again, again kindly, and he said,
"I am Miriam's nephew, dear. I'm living here until
I get her affairs in order."

"Oh."

I couldn't think of anything else to say.

Then Cletus said, "Where are the bats?"

The chipmunk chuckled. He said, "Flying free, son. Like the Reverend Young herself."

All this time Ob had said nothing. He hadn't even been facing us. As soon as he'd learned Reverend Young was dead, he had turned away and looked off the side of the porch, rubbing his forehead as he always did when he was lost and searching for a way to go.

But after the feeble attempts of Cletus and me to deal with this house empty of its Small Medium at Large, he turned back. Turned back and in a quiet voice said to the man, "I was hoping she could help me contact my wife. I needed to talk to my wife."

And the nephew of the preacher Ob had needed so desperately to find looked on Ob's heart-broken face and saw his pain and he reached out and put a hand on Ob's shoulder.

"I am so sorry, sir, but I haven't my aunt's spiritual powers. There is no one else here. But I do know someone, a man in Sissonville, who might be able to . . ."

But Ob put up his hand and shook his head.

"No," he said. "No. We were led here, and here my looking ends. I can't go traipsing through the state like some old fool, searching out psychics. I'm not meant to do it and I won't."

Cletus looked at me and I looked at him, both of us hoping for the other one to do something.

Then Cletus said, "Well, sir, do you have any materials you might give us? Anything she might have used in church?"

Leave it to Cletus to think of that. Wanting something to take, something to hold between his fingers, to hide away in his vinyl suitcase. Cletus always needing something to collect.

"Well," said the nephew, "there is the church brochure the Reverend always handed out to newcomers. I could give you one of those."

Cletus nodded his head.

The nephew looked over at Ob.

"Would you care to come inside while I look? Could I offer you a cup of coffee?"

But Ob shook his head and remained silent. His face was pale and full of strain, and I wanted to take his suffering from him. But all I could do was wait for the chipmunk and Cletus to take care of their business so we might just go on home.

The nephew reappeared at the door with a folded white paper in his hands. He again apologized sorrowfully, wrote his number on the paper in case he could ever be of any help to us, and then the door that had held so much hope was closed and we were back on our own again.

We walked silently to the Valiant, then sat there a few minutes without a word. I was waiting for Ob to decide what he was going to do next. We had already called up our reservations at the one motel in town. Then tomorrow—after the Reverend Young would have connected Ob to May and everything was finally set right—tomorrow we were supposed to drive to the capitol. Spend the whole day there hobnobbing with the legislators. And then we were to go home and maybe live again.

But it was only eleven o'clock in the morning, we had been on this journey only three hours, and already everything was cracked and broken—and some of us with it.

Ob gave a deep sigh and he said, "I guess we better head on home, children."

He started the car, and slowly we pulled away from all the spirits resting in that little blue house. Cletus and I said nothing. I guess we both knew it was too delicate a situation for fixing.

Unlike the happy silence we'd all enjoyed earlier that morning, we suffered instead a black kind of stillness on our route back home. Ob looked awful. I thought he might just pull the car over to the shoulder and die. Cletus opened up the Spiritualist handout and stared at the page mile after mile. And I watched out my window, swallowing back the lump in my throat and praying for something to save Ob and me. For I truly felt Ob had taken his final punch.

Off of I–64 and back on the turnpike, the signs for Capitol Street started cropping up again. I could feel Cletus lift his eyes and watch them slide past. And before long, there she was. That pretty concrete queen Cletus wanted to marry someday.

We traveled the road up the river alongside her, and no one said a word. My heart was aching for Cletus, for I knew there was little in life he really wanted this bad, this chance to see the West Virginia State Capitol. But I had nothing left to try to get it for him. We headed on south toward the bridge that would take us across the river and as far away from Cletus's capitol as any soul could be. Back to Deep Water, where life would become again an empty trailer, an old man's declining will to go on, a crazy fool believing in the mysteries of a beat-up vinyl suitcase, and me. I kept my eyes straight ahead, unwilling to look behind me at that gold shining dome that had accepted all our deepest wishes just a few hours back. Then just as we were nearly out of its sight, just as we were ready to put that last disappointment behind us and go back to the old life, we heard Ob say, "I'm turning this buggy around."

And he did. He turned that buggy around and he drove it back the way we'd come. Back toward that shining castle. My heart began to lift. And Cletus leaned forward from the backseat.

Sounding almost too scared to ask, he said, "Are we going anyway, Ob? Going in to see it?"

Ob said, "It's getting on to lunchtime. I figure the governor will be in the coffee shop, watching for somebody interesting to come through the door."

Ob straightened his shoulders, and his face eased up a little, and he said, "We sure don't want to disappoint him."

CHAPTER ELEVEN

*M*ay always said we were angels before we were ever people. She said
when we were finished being people we'd go back
to being angels. And we'd never feel pain again.

But what is it that makes a person want to stay
here on this earth anyway, and go on suffering the
most awful pain just for the sake of getting to stay?

I used to think it was because people fear
death. But now I think it is because people can't
bear saying good-bye.

May was lucky. When she had to say her good-
bye to Ob, she had to hurt over it only once. And
then she was an angel and it didn't hurt her anymore.

But Ob. Ob hurt and he kept on hurting. Living

in a trailer full of May's empty spaces. Walking through May's dying garden. Sleeping in a bed that still left room for her.

He hurt so much. But even after his most terrible hours, he decided to stay here on this earth. Right out of the blue, he wanted to live again. And I'd like to think maybe he wanted to live because of me. Because he couldn't bear the thought of saying good-bye to me.

Something happened to Ob that day we left Putnam County and started back for home. Between the front porch of the late Reverend Young's and the concrete steps of the West Virginia State Capitol, something happened to Ob to make him long for living again. I don't know what it was. I couldn't even take any credit for making it happen when it did. I figured Ob had given up there on that porch in Putnam County and I was preparing myself for the worst. But something happened to Ob. He turned that buggy around.

The three of us found an easy place to park right beside the capitol building and we got out of the car and walked into that place like three people coming home. We didn't feel small. We didn't mind that we were new. We felt embraced and even sort of expected.

Cletus seemed to need to touch everything. Even when we walked down the halls, he'd run his fingers lightly against the walls. We stopped at every lighted display window. We read the name on every door. We picked up every brochure. And Cletus smiled at each person we passed as if he knew everyone well.

And all this time Ob was gentle with him and with me, gentle like a mother. He would lean with Cletus over a glass case in the museum, and his arm would lie softly about Cletus's shoulders as they read the words off an old yellowed newspaper. And while I stood in front of a beautiful window, looking out at the capitol lawn with its pigeons and squirrels and pretty women walking together and laughing, Ob would stand beside me and rest his palm against the back of my head as he used to when I was a little girl.

In the capitol coffee shop we looked for signs of the governor, but I guess he was off somewhere else that day. So we just eavesdropped on the conversations of all the other men and women in their nice suits, people who had come downstairs from their big offices with leather chairs to have a cup of capitol coffee and relax. Cletus watched them with a kind of ache in his eyes, and I knew what he wanted for his life and I prayed for him to someday get it. But I didn't say any prayers for me. I was too afraid to hope for things.

We went through every bit of space in the capitol building that we could find; then we went next door to the Science and Culture Center and soaked in all of that place, too. There was a gift shop there selling handmade items by West Virginians, and it was Cletus who said that Ob ought to be bringing in his whirligigs to sell. I could see that Ob actually gave it some thought. He looked around the shop like somebody planning out a garden they're about to plant. He'd stare at one corner, then another, like he was setting up his whirligigs there, in his head, getting the feel of it.

But when we walked out of the shop, Ob said to Cletus, "My 'gigs are needing a place. This ain't it."

We stayed among the senators and legislators until five o'clock, and when they started heading out to their cars to go home, we called the Glen Meadows Motel to cancel; then we headed on out to ours. I gave Cletus the front seat.

It was dark when we finally pulled into the yard, the headlights of the car flashing across Ob's old Chevy sitting in the weeds. We'd been quiet all the way home, but not a hard, lonely quiet. Just tired. Full of thoughts.

We were getting ourselves and our stuff out of the car. Ob was talking to Cletus about how comfy the couch was to sleep on (Ob had asked Cletus to spend the night so we wouldn't have to answer any awkward questions from Cletus's parents). And I was thinking of May.

Then something flew over me.

We all let out a little gasp. The wings were so completely silent and we so unprepared. But the moon was bright and the shadow of those wings so real, and before we could find our voices, before I could call out, "Wait!" the owl had flown off into the night.

I remembered her then. I remembered May.

I began to cry. I had not ever really cried for May. I had tried so hard to bear her loss and had swallowed back the tears that had been building up inside me for two seasons. But nothing could keep them back once that owl disappeared from my eyes and I knew as I had never known before that I would never, ever, see May on this earth again.

I cried and cried and could not stop crying. Then Ob lifted me up and carried me through the door Cletus held open and he took me to my room as he had done so many times when I was a little girl. My stomach and my throat burned and ached with the tears as I curled into a ball on my bed and tried to cry the very life out of my body. But for every bit of life I cried away, Ob held me hard against him and he put more life back in me. He did not ever speak. Just held on to me and wiped away the tears with his strong, wide hands until finally my body was emptied of those tears and I was no more burdened.

When finally I felt I could speak, I whispered to him, "It's been so hard missing May."

And Ob said, "She's still here, honey. People don't ever leave us for good."

I laid my head on his shoulder, so grateful he was still here with me, grateful even for Cletus, who I knew was somewhere in the trailer, waiting. I closed my eyes and thought of my poor young mama and May's poor mommy and daddy and my dear May herself. But I didn't dwell on them with pain or with fear. There was a tranquillity in me that felt all right, and as I remembered them all, my tears dried up and I fell asleep.

When Ob and me met you, honey, you was such a shy thing. Them big ol' eyes of yours looking like a puppy begging for love.

I knew right off I wanted you. I took Ob out to the back porch after supper and I said, "Ob, we've got to take that child home with us."

Well, Ob had seen how at the supper table you'd been too scared to death to ask for anything. Run out of milk in your glass and too scared to ask Connie Francine to fill it up again. Ob knew an unhappy child when he saw one.

So he said, "We're taking her today, May," and we just packed you up and took you. Those folks never cared. Those Ohio kin—they're good people mostly, but they're limited, honey.

I couldn't hardly keep my hands off you those first few days. Remember how I was always touching your hair, combing it all the time and clipping pretty bows to it? I had me a little girl finally, something I'd wanted all my life. I'd come to figure the good Lord wasn't ever going to give me one, for reasons of His own. But He was holding me steady all those years, waiting for you to be born, waiting for your poor mama to die, waiting for Ob to see you didn't know how to ask for a glass of milk.

I worried about us not having the money to give you all you truly deserved. I wanted so much to buy you them big plastic houses with those little round-headed people sitting inside. And those great big baby dolls that wet their diapers. I wanted to dress you up in pink and yellow every day. Take you over to Charleston to that big glass mall and go in that big department store and buy everything pink and yellow for little girls.

But we just didn't have much, honey. We were both sorry for it. Ob made you those little wooden people to play with. And I picked through everything at the Goodwill to find you some nice clothes. But we knew you should've had more. We were so sorry for it.

Remember you and me out late that one night? What is it we were doing. . . . You thought you heard a cat a-meowing and wanted me to come see with you. Do you remember? And we put on our coats and went out, and the moon was as big around as I'd ever seen it, and we didn't need no lights, it was that bright. And just as we were heading for the shed to see if there was a lost kitty in there somewhere, out of that dark came a big owl just swooping right across our path. Biggest thing I'd ever seen, and not a sound. And you and me, we couldn't say a word. Just stood there with our hands over our mouths, frozen up like statues, watching those wings flap off into the dark.

I'd not ever seen an owl in all my days, and when I hadn't had you but a few weeks there that one passed through my life. I knew you'd always be doing that for me and for Ob. Bringing us good things like that.

I used to wonder why God gave you to us so late in life. Why we had to be old already before we could have you. I was almost big as a house and full of diabetes. And Ob an old arthritic skeleton of a man. We couldn't do none of the things we could've done for you thirty or forty years back.

But I thought on it and thought on it till I finally figured it out.

And my guess is that the Lord wanted us all to be

just full of need. If Ob and me had been young and strong, why, maybe you wouldn't've felt so necessary to us. Maybe you'd've thought we could do just fine without you.

So the Lord let us get old so we'd have plenty cause to need you and you'd feel free to need us right back. We wanted a family so bad, all of us. And we just grabbed onto each another and made us one. Simple as that.

I always told Ob he was my moon and sun. And when you came to us, Summer, honey, you were my shining star.

You are the best little girl I ever did know.

CHAPTER TWELVE

When I opened my eyes the next morning, the brightest yellow sunshine was coming through the window. It is nearly spring now. May's daffodils will be blooming.

I smelled hot coffee brewing in the kitchen, and bacon. Somebody was cooking me breakfast.

I came out of my room to find Cletus setting the table and telling Ob all about some article he'd read on people spontaneously combusting. And Ob cracking eggs into a big plastic bowl and telling Cletus he didn't believe a word of it.

I said, "Good morning," and they both grinned at me and said good morning back. Then we all three ate ourselves nearly to oblivion on the best eggs and bacon I ever tasted in my life.

After breakfast Ob said, "I got us all a chore this morning."

And within minutes we were carrying whirligigs out the door.

We used May's tomato stakes and other bits of board we could find and we filled up May's empty garden with Dreams and Thunderstorms and Fire and that bright white Spirit that was May herself. Then Cletus went inside the trailer and came out carrying the Reverend Young's church handout.

We stood there in May's beloved and practical garden, and Cletus searched the handout for some good words to say to bless the whirligigs that now had a place to spin and fly and live.

He read:

" 'What is the true mission of spirit messages? To bring us consolation in the sorrows of life....' "

Ob and I smiled at each other. And then a big wind came and set everything free.

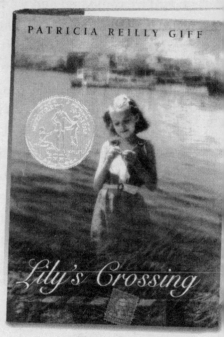